SJAMBAK

SJAMBAK

JACK VANCE

WILDSIDE PRESS

SJAMBAK

Originally published in *If Worlds of Science Fiction*, July 1953 issue.
Frontispiece by Virgil Finlay.

SJAMBAK

HOWARD FRAYBERG, Production Director of *Know Your Universe!*, was a man of sudden unpredictable moods; and Sam Catlin, the show's Continuity Editor, had learned to expect the worst.

"Sam," said Frayberg, "regarding the show last night. . . ." He paused to seek the proper words, and Catlin relaxed. Frayberg's frame of mind was merely critical. "Sam, we're in a rut. What's worse, the show's dull!"

Sam Catlin shrugged, not committing himself.

"Seaweed Processors of Alphard IX—who cares about seaweed?"

"It's factual stuff," said Sam, defensive but not wanting to go too far out on a limb. "We bring 'em everything—color, fact, romance, sight, sound, smell. . . . Next week, it's the Ball Expedition to the Mixtup Mountains on Gropus."

Frayberg leaned forward. "Sam, we're working the wrong slant on this stuff. . . . We've got to loosen up, sock 'em! Shift our ground! Give 'em the old human angle—glamor, mystery, thrills!"

Sam Catlin curled his lips. "I got just what you want."

"Yeah? Show me."

Catlin reached into his waste basket. "I filed this just ten minutes ago. . . ." He smoothed out the pages. "'Sequence idea, by Wilbur Murphy. Investigate "Horseman of Space," the man who rides up to meet incoming space-ships.'"

Frayberg tilted his head to the side. "Rides up on a *horse*?"

"That's what Wilbur Murphy says."

"How far up?"

"Does it make any difference?"

"No—I guess not."

"Well, for your information, it's up ten thousand, twenty thousand miles. He waves to the pilot, takes off his hat to the passengers, then rides back down."

"And where does all this take place?"

"On—on—" Catlin frowned. "I can write it, but I can't pronounce it." He printed on his scratch-screen: CIRGAMESÇ.

"Sirgamesk," read Frayberg.

Catlin shook his head. "That's what it looks like—but those consonants are all aspirated gutturals. It's more like 'Hrrghameshgrrh'."

"Where did Murphy get this tip?"

"I didn't bother to ask."

"Well," mused Frayberg, "we could always do a show on strange superstitions. Is Murphy around?"

"He's explaining his expense account to Shifkin."

"Get him in here; let's talk to him."

WILBUR MURPHY had a blond crew-cut, a broad freckled nose, and a serious sidelong squint. He looked from his crumpled sequence idea to Catlin and Frayberg. "Didn't like it, eh?"

"We thought the emphasis should be a little different," explained Catlin. "Instead of 'The Space Horseman,' we'd give it the working title, 'Odd Superstitions of Hrrghameshgrrh'."

"Oh, hell!" said Frayberg. "Call it Sirgamesk."

"Anyway," said Catlin, "that's the angle."

"But it's not superstition," said Murphy.

"Oh, come, Wilbur . . ."

"I got this for sheer sober-sided fact. A man rides a horse up to meet the incoming ships!"

"Where did you get this wild fable?"

"My brother-in-law is purser on the *Celestial Traveller*. At Riker's Planet they make connection with the feeder line out of Cirgamesç."

"Wait a minute," said Catlin. "How did you pronounce that?"

"Cirgamesç. The steward on the shuttle-ship gave out this story, and my brother-in-law passed it along to me."

"Somebody's pulling somebody's leg."

"My brother-in-law wasn't, and the steward was cold sober."

"They've been eating *bhang*. Sirgamesk is a Javanese planet, isn't it?"

"Javanese, Arab, Malay."

"Then they took a *bhang* supply with them, and *hashish*, *chat*, and a few other sociable herbs."

"Well, this horseman isn't any drug-dream."

"No? What is it?"

"So far as I know it's a man on a horse."

"Ten thousand miles up? In a vacuum?"

"Exactly."

"No space-suit?"

"That's the story."

Catlin and Frayberg looked at each other.

"Well, Wilbur," Catlin began.

Frayberg interrupted. "What we can use, Wilbur, is a sequence on Sirgamesk superstition. Emphasis on voodoo or witchcraft—naked girls dancing—stuff with roots in Earth, but now typically Sirgamesk. Lots of color. Secret rite stuff. . . ."

"Not much room on Cirgamesç for secret rites."

"It's a big planet, isn't it?"

"Not quite as big as Mars. There's no atmosphere. The settlers live in mountain valleys, with air-tight lids over 'em."

Catlin flipped the pages of *Thumbnail Sketches of the Inhabited Worlds.* "Says here there's ancient ruins millions of years old. When the atmosphere went, the population went with it."

Frayberg became animated. "There's lots of material out there! Go get it, Wilbur! Life! Sex! Excitement! Mystery!"

"Okay," said Wilbur Murphy.

"But lay off this horseman-in-space. There *is* a limit to public credulity, and don't you let anyone tell you different."

CIRGAMESÇ hung outside the port, twenty thousand miles ahead. The steward leaned over Wilbur Murphy's shoulder and pointed a long brown finger. "It was right out there, sir. He came riding up—"

"What kind of a man was it? Strange-looking?"

"No. He was Cirgameski."

"Oh. You saw him with your own eyes, eh?"

The steward bowed, and his loose white mantle fell forward. "Exactly, sir."

"No helmet, no space-suit?"

"He wore a short Singhalût vest and pantaloons and a yellow Hadrasi hat. No more."

"And the horse?"

"Ah, the horse! There's a different matter."

"Different how?"

"I can't describe the horse. I was intent on the man."

"Did you recognize him?"

"By the brow of Lord Allah, it's well not to look too closely when such matters occur."

"Then—you *did* recognize him!"

"I must be at my task, sir."

Murphy frowned in vexation at the steward's retreating back, then bent over his camera to check the tape-feed. If anything appeared now, and his eyes could see it, the two-hundred million audience of *Know Your Universe!* could see it with him.

When he looked up, Murphy made a frantic grab for the stanchion, then relaxed. Cirgamesç had taken the Great Twitch. It was an illusion, a psychological quirk. One instant the planet lay ahead; then a man winked or turned away, and when he looked back, "ahead" had become "below"; the planet had swung an astonishing ninety degrees across the sky, and they were *falling*!

Murphy leaned against the stanchion. "'The Great Twitch'," he muttered to himself, "I'd like to get *that* on two hundred million screens!"

Several hours passed. Cirgamesç grew. The Sampan Range rose up like a dark scab; the valley sultanates of Singhalût, Hadra, New Batavia, and Boeng-Bohôt showed like glistening chicken-tracks; the Great Rift Colony of Sundaman stretched down through the foothills like the trail of a slug.

A loudspeaker voice rattled the ship. "Attention passengers for Singhalût and other points on Cirgamesç! Kindly prepare your luggage for disembarkation. Customs at Singhalût are extremely thorough. Passengers are warned to take no weapons, drugs or explosives ashore. This is important!"

THE WARNING turned out to be an understatement. Murphy was plied with questions. He suffered search of an intimate nature. He was three-dimensionally X-rayed with a range of frequencies calculated to excite fluorescence in whatever object he might have secreted in his stomach, in a hollow bone, or under a layer of flesh.

His luggage was explored with similar minute attention, and Murphy rescued his cameras with difficulty. "What're you so damn anxious about? I don't have drugs; I don't have contraband . . ."

"It's guns, your excellency. Guns, weapons, explosives . . ."

"I don't have any guns."

"But these objects here?"

"They're cameras. They record pictures and sounds and smells."

The inspector seized the cases with a glittering smile of triumph. "They resemble no cameras of my experience; I fear I shall have to impound . . ."

A young man in loose white pantaloons, a pink vest, pale green cravat and a complex black turban strolled up. The inspector made a swift obeisance, with arms spread wide. "Excellency."

The young man raised two fingers. "You may find it possible to spare Mr. Murphy any unnecessary formality."

"As your Excellency recommends. . . ." The inspector nimbly repacked Murphy's belongings, while the young man looked on benignly.

Murphy covertly inspected his face. The skin was smooth, the color of the rising moon; the eyes were narrow, dark, superficially placid. The effect was of silken punctilio with hot ruby blood close beneath.

Satisfied with the inspector's zeal, he turned to Murphy. "Allow me to introduce myself, Tuan Murphy. I am Ali-Tomás, of the House of Singhalût, and my father the Sultan begs you to accept our poor hospitality."

"Why, thank you," said Murphy. "This is a very pleasant surprise."

"If you will allow me to conduct you. . . ." He turned to the inspector. "Mr. Murphy's luggage to the palace."

MURPHY accompanied Ali-Tomás into the outside light, fitting his own quick step to the prince's feline saunter. This is coming it pretty soft, he said to himself. I'll have a magnificent suite, with bowls of fruit and gin pahits, not to mention two or three silken girls with skin like rich cream bringing me towels in the shower. . . . Well, well, well, it's not so bad working for *Know Your Universe!* after all! I suppose I ought to unlimber my camera. . . .

Prince Ali-Tomás watched him with interest. "And what is the audience of *Know Your Universe!*?"

"We call 'em 'participants'."

"Expressive. And how many participants do you serve?"

"Oh, the Bowdler Index rises and falls. We've got about two hundred million screens, with five hundred million participants."

"Fascinating! And tell me—how do you record smells?"

Murphy displayed the odor recorder on the side of the camera, with its gelatinous track which fixed the molecular design.

"And the odors recreated—they are like the originals?"

"Pretty close. Never exact, but none of the participants knows the difference. Sometimes the synthetic odor is an improvement."

"Astounding!" murmured the prince.

"And sometimes . . . Well, Carson Tenlake went out to get the myrrh-blossoms on Venus. It was a hot day—as days usually are on Venus—and a long climb. When the show was run off, there was more smell of Carson than of flowers."

Prince Ali-Tomás laughed politely. "We turn through here."

They came out into a compound paved with red, green and white tiles. Beneath the valley roof was a sinuous trough, full of haze and warmth and golden light. As far in either direction as the eye could reach, the hillsides were terraced, barred in various shades of green. Spattering the valley floor were tall canvas pavilions, tents, booths, shelters.

"Naturally," said Prince Ali-Tomás, "we hope that you and your participants will enjoy Singhalût. It is a truism that, in order to import, we must export; we wish to encourage a pleasurable response to the 'Made in Singhalût' tag on our *batiks*, carvings, lacquers."

They rolled quietly across the square in a surface-car displaying the House emblem. Murphy rested against deep, cool cushions. "Your inspectors are pretty careful about weapons."

Ali-Tomás smiled complacently. "Our existence is ordered and peaceful. You may be familiar with the concept of *adak*?"

"I don't think so."

"A word, an idea from old Earth. Every living act is ordered by ritual. But our heritage is passionate—and when unyielding *adak* stands in the way of an irresistible emotion, there is turbulence, sometimes even killing."

"An *amok*."

"Exactly. It is as well that the *amok* has no weapons other than his knife. Otherwise he would kill twenty where now he kills one."

The car rolled along a narrow avenue, scattering pedestrians to either side like the bow of a boat spreading foam. The men wore loose white pantaloons and a short open vest; the women wore only the pantaloons.

"Handsome set of people," remarked Murphy.

Ali-Tomás again smiled complacently. "I'm sure Singhalût will present an inspiring and beautiful spectacle for your program."

Murphy remembered the keynote to Howard Frayberg's instructions: "*Excitement! Sex! Mystery!*" Frayberg cared little for inspiration or beauty. "I imagine," he said casually, "that you celebrate a number of interesting festivals? Colorful dancing? Unique customs?"

Ali-Tomás shook his head. "To the contrary. We left our superstitions and ancestor-worship back on Earth. We are quiet Mohammedans and indulge in very little festivity. Perhaps here is the reason for *amoks* and sjambaks."

"Sjambaks?"

"We are not proud of them. You will hear sly rumor, and it is better that I arm you beforehand with truth."

"What is a sjambak?"

"They are bandits, flouters of authority. I will show you one presently."

"I heard," said Murphy, "of a man riding a horse up to meet the space-ships. What would account for a story like that?"

"It can have no possible basis," said Prince Ali-Tomás. "We have no horses on Cirgamesç. None whatever."

"But . . ."

"The veriest idle talk. Such nonsense will have no interest for your intelligent participants."

The car rolled into a square a hundred yards on a side, lined with luxuriant banana palms. Opposite was an enormous pavilion of gold and violet silk, with a dozen peaked gables casting various changing sheens. In the center of the square a twenty-foot pole supported a cage about two feet wide, three feet long, and four feet high.

Inside this cage crouched a naked man.

The car rolled past. Prince Ali-Tomás waved an idle hand. The caged man glared down from bloodshot eyes. "That," said Ali-Tomás, "is a sjambak. As you see," a faint note of apology entered his voice, "we attempt to discourage them."

"What's that metal object on his chest?"

"The mark of his trade. By that you may know all sjambak. In these unsettled times only we of the House may cover our chests—all others must show themselves and declare themselves true Singhalûsi."

Murphy said tentatively, "I must come back here and photograph that cage."

Ali-Tomás smilingly shook his head. "I will show you our farms, our vines and orchards. Your participants will enjoy these; they have no interest in the dolor of an ignoble sjambak."

"Well," said Murphy, "our aim is a well-rounded production. We want to show the farmers at work, the members of the great House at their responsibilities, as well as the deserved fate of wrongdoers."

"Exactly. For every sjambak there are ten thousand industrious Singhalûsi. It follows then that only one ten-thousandth part of your film should be devoted to this infamous minority."

"About three-tenths of a second, eh?"

"No more than they deserve."

"You don't know my Production Director. His name is Howard Frayberg, and . . ."

HOWARD FRAYBERG was deep in conference with Sam Catlin, under the influence of what Catlin called his philosophic kick. It was the phase which Catlin feared most.

"Sam," said Frayberg, "do you know the danger of this business?"

"Ulcers," Catlin replied promptly.

Frayberg shook his head. "We've got an occupational disease to fight—progressive mental myopia."

"Speak for yourself," said Catlin.

"Consider. We sit in this office. We think we know what kind of show we want. We send out our staff to get it. We're signing the checks, so back it comes the way we asked for it. We look at it, hear it, smell it—and pretty soon we believe it: our version of the universe, full-blown from our brains like Minerva stepping out of Zeus. You see what I mean?"

"I understand the words."

"We've got our own picture of what's going on. We ask for it, we get it. It builds up and up—and finally we're like mice in a trap built of our own ideas. We cannibalize our own brains."

"Nobody'll ever accuse you of being stingy with a metaphor."

"Sam, let's have the truth. How many times have you been off Earth?"

"I went to Mars once. And I spent a couple of weeks at Aristillus Resort on the Moon."

Frayberg leaned back in his chair as if shocked. "And we're supposed to be a couple of learned planetologists!"

Catlin made grumbling noise in his throat. "I haven't been around the zodiac, so what? You sneezed a few minutes ago and I said *gesundheit*, but I don't have any doctor's degree."

"There comes a time in a man's life," said Frayberg, "when he wants to take stock, get a new perspective."

"Relax, Howard, relax."

"In our case it means taking out our preconceived ideas, looking at them, checking our illusions against reality."

"Are you serious about this?"

"Another thing," said Frayberg, "I want to check up a little. Shifkin says the expense accounts are frightful. But he can't fight it. When Keeler says he paid ten munits for a loaf of bread on Nekkar IV, who's gonna call him on it?"

"Hell, let him eat bread! That's cheaper than making a safari around the cluster, spot-checking the super-markets."

Frayberg paid no heed. He touched a button; a three-foot sphere full of glistening motes appeared. Earth was at the center, with thin red lines, the scheduled space-ship routes, radiating out in all directions.

"Let's see what kind of circle we can make," said Frayberg. "Gower's here at Canopus, Keeler's over here at Blue Moon, Wilbur Murphy's at Sirgamesk . . . ."

"Don't forget," muttered Catlin, "we got a show to put on."

"We've got material for a year," scoffed Frayberg. "Get hold of Space-Lines. We'll start with Sirgamesk, and see what Wilbur Murphy's up to."

WILBUR MURPHY was being presented to the Sultan of Singhalût by the Prince Ali-Tomás. The Sultan, a small mild man of seventy, sat crosslegged on an enormous pink and green air-cushion. "Be at your ease, Mr. Murphy. We dispense with as much protocol here as practicable." The Sultan had a dry clipped voice and the air of a rather harassed corporation executive. "I understand you represent Earth-Central Home Screen Network?"

"I'm a staff photographer for the *Know Your Universe!* show."

"We export a great deal to Earth," mused the Sultan, "but not as much as we'd like. We're very pleased with your interest in us, and naturally we want to help you in every way possible. Tomorrow the Keeper of the Archives will present a series of charts analyzing our economy. Ali-Tomás shall personally conduct you through the fish-hatcheries. We want you to know we're doing a great job out here on Singhalût."

"I'm sure you are," said Murphy uncomfortably. "However, that isn't quite the stuff I want."

"No? Just where do your desires lie?"

Ali-Tomás said delicately. "Mr. Murphy took a rather profound interest in the sjambak displayed in the square."

"Oh. And you explained that these renegades could hold no interest for serious students of our planet?"

Murphy started to explain that clustered around two hundred million screens tuned to *Know Your Universe!* were four or five hundred million participants, the greater part of them neither serious nor students. The Sultan cut in decisively. "I will now impart something truly interesting. We Singhalûsi are making preparations to reclaim four more valleys, with an added area of six hundred thousand acres! I shall put my physiographic models at your disposal; you may use them to the fullest extent!"

"I'll be pleased for the opportunity," declared Murphy. "But tomorrow I'd like to prowl around the valley, meet your people, observe their customs, religious rites, courtships, funerals . . ."

The Sultan pulled a sour face. "We are ditch-water dull. Festivals are celebrated quietly in the home; there is small religious fervor; courtships are consummated by family contract. I fear you will find little sensational material here in Singhalût."

"You have no temple dances?" asked Murphy. "No fire-walkers, snake-charmers—voodoo?"

The Sultan smiled patronizingly. "We came out here to Cirgamesç to escape the ancient superstitions. Our lives are calm, orderly. Even the *amoks* have practically disappeared."

"But the sjambaks—"

"Negligible."

"Well," said Murphy, "I'd like to visit some of these ancient cities."

"I advise against it," declared the Sultan. "They are shards, weathered stone. There are no inscriptions, no art. There is no stimulation in dead stone. Now. Tomorrow I will hear a report on hybrid soybean plantings in the Upper Kam District. You will want to be present."

MURPHY'S SUITE matched or even excelled his expectation. He had four rooms and a private garden enclosed by a thicket of bamboo. His bathroom walls were slabs of glossy actinolite, inlaid with cinnabar, jade, galena, pyrite and blue malachite, in representations of fantastic birds. His bedroom was a tent thirty feet high. Two walls were dark green fabric; a third was golden rust; the fourth opened upon the private garden.

Murphy's bed was a pink and yellow creation ten feet square, soft as cobweb, smelling of rose sandalwood. Carved black lacquer tubs held fruit; two dozen wines, liquors, syrups, essences flowed at a touch from as many ebony spigots.

The garden centered on a pool of cool water, very pleasant in the hothouse climate of Singhalût. The only shortcoming was the lack of the lovely young servitors Murphy had envisioned. He took it upon himself to repair this lack, and in a shady wine-house behind the palace, called the Barangipan, he made the acquaintance of a girl-musician named Soek Panjoebang. He found her enticing tones of quavering sweetness from the *gamelan*, an instrument well-loved in Old Bali. Soek Panjoebang had the delicate features and transparent skin of Sumatra, the supple long limbs of Arabia and in a pair of wide and golden eyes a heritage from somewhere in Celtic Europe. Murphy bought her a goblet of frozen shavings, each a different perfume, while he himself drank white rice-beer. Soek Panjoebang displayed an intense interest in the ways of Earth, and Murphy found it hard to guide the conversation. "Weelbrrr," she said. "Such a funny name, Weelbrrr. Do you think I could play the *gamelan* in the great cities, the great palaces of Earth?"

"Sure. There's no law against *gamelans*."

"You talk so funny, Weelbrrr. I like to hear you talk."

"I suppose you get kinda bored here in Singhalût?"

She shrugged. "Life is pleasant, but it concerns with little things. We have no great adventures. We grow flowers, we play the *gamelan*." She eyed him archly sidelong. "We love. . . . We sleep. . . ."

Murphy grinned. "You run *amok*."

"No, no, no. That is no more."

"Not since the sjambaks, eh?"

"The sjambaks are bad. But better than *amok*. When a man feels the knot forming around his chest, he no longer takes his kris and runs down the street—he becomes sjambak."

This was getting interesting. "Where does he go? What does he do?"

"He robs."

"Who does he rob? What does he do with his loot?"

She leaned toward him. "It is not well to talk of them."

"Why not?"

"The Sultan does not wish it. Everywhere are listeners. When one talks sjambak, the Sultan's ears rise, like the points on a cat."

"Suppose they do—what's the difference? I've got a legitimate in-terest. I saw one of them in that cage out there. That's torture. I want to know about it."

"He is very bad. He opened the monorail car and the air rushed out. Forty-two Singhalûsi and Hadrasi bloated and blew up."

"And what happened to the sjambak?"

"He took all the gold and money and jewels and ran away."

"Ran where?"

"Out across Great Pharasang Plain. But he was a fool. He came back to Singhalût for his wife; he was caught and set up for all people to look at, so they might tell each other, 'thus it is for sjambaks.'"

"Where do the sjambaks hide out?"

"Oh," she looked vaguely around the room, "out on the plains. In the mountains."

"They must have some shelter—an air-dome."

"No. The Sultan would send out his patrol-boat and destroy them. They roam quietly. They hide among the rocks and tend their oxygen stills. Sometimes they visit the old cities."

"I wonder," said Murphy, staring into his beer, "could it be sjambaks who ride horses up to meet the space-ship?"

Soek Panjoebang knit her black eyebrows, as if preoccupied.

"That's what brought me out here," Murphy went on. "This story of a man riding a horse out in space."

"Ridiculous; we have no horses in Cirgamesç."

"All right, the steward won't swear to the horse. Suppose the man was up there on foot or riding a bicycle. But the steward recognized the man."

"Who was this man, pray?"

"The steward clammed up. . . . The name would have been just noise to me, anyway."

"*I* might recognize the name. . . ."

"Ask him yourself. The ship's still out at the field."

She shook her head slowly, holding her golden eyes on his face. "I do not care to attract the attention of either steward, sjambak—or Sultan."

Murphy said impatiently. "In any event, it's not who—but *how*. How does the man breathe? Vacuum sucks a man's lungs up out of his mouth, bursts his stomach, his ears. . . ."

"We have excellent doctors," said Soek Panjoebang shuddering, "but alas! I am not one of them."

MURPHY LOOKED at her sharply. Her voice held the plangent sweetness of her instrument, with additional overtones of mockery. "There must be some kind of invisible dome around him, holding in air," said Murphy.

"And what if there is?"

"It's something new, and if it is, I want to find out about it."

Soek smiled languidly. "You are so typical an old-lander—worried, frowning, dynamic. You should relax, cultivate *napaû*, enjoy life as we do here in Singhalût."

"What's *napaû*?"

"It's our philosophy, where we find meaning and life and beauty in every aspect of the world."

"That sjambak in the cage could do with a little less *napaû* right now."

"No doubt he is unhappy," she agreed.

"Unhappy! He's being tortured!"

"He broke the Sultan's law. His life is no longer his own. It belongs to Singhalût. If the Sultan wishes to use it to warn other wrongdoers, the fact that the man suffers is of small interest."

"If they all wear that metal ornament, how can they hope to hide out?" He glanced at her own bare bosom.

"They appear by night—slip through the streets like ghosts. . . ." She looked in turn at Murphy's loose shirt. "You will notice persons brushing up against you, feeling you," she laid her hand along his breast, "and when this happens you will know they are agents of the Sultan, because only strangers and the House may wear shirts. But now, let me sing to you—a song from the Old Land, old Java. You will not understand the tongue, but no other words so join the voice of the *gamelan*."

"THIS IS the gravy-train," said Murphy. "Instead of a garden suite with a private pool, I usually sleep in a bubble-tent, with nothing to eat but condensed food."

Soek Panjoebang flung the water out of her sleek black hair. "Perhaps, Weelbrrr, you will regret leaving Cirgamesç?"

"Well," he looked up to the transparent roof, barely visible where the sunlight collected and refracted, "I don't particularly like being shut up like a bird in an aviary. . . . Mildly claustrophobic, I guess."

After breakfast, drinking thick coffee from tiny silver cups, Murphy looked long and reflectively at Soek Panjoebang.

"What are you thinking, Weelbrrr?"

Murphy drained his coffee. "I'm thinking that I'd better be getting to work."

"And what do you do?"

"First I'm going to shoot the palace, and you sitting here in the garden playing your *gamelan*."

"But Weelbrrr—not *me*!"

"You're a part of the universe, rather an interesting part. Then I'll take the square. . . ."

"And the sjambak?"

A quiet voice spoke from behind. "A visitor, Tuan Murphy."

Murphy turned his head. "Bring him in." He looked back to Soek Panjoebang. She was on her feet.

"It is necessary that I go."

"When will I see you?"

"Tonight—at the Barangipan."

* * * * *

THE QUIET VOICE said, "Mr. Rube Trimmer, Tuan."

Trimmer was small and middle-aged, with thin shoulders and a paunch. He carried himself with a hell-raising swagger, left over from a time twenty years gone. His skin had the waxy look of lost floridity, his tuft of white hair was coarse and thin, his eyelids hung in the off-side droop that amateur physiognomists like to associate with guile.

"I'm Resident Director of the Import-Export Bank," said Trimmer. "Heard you were here and thought I'd pay my respects."

"I suppose you don't see many strangers."

"Not too many—there's nothing much to bring 'em. Cirgamesç isn't a comfortable tourist planet. Too confined, shut in. A man with a sensitive psyche goes nuts pretty easy here."

"Yeah," said Murphy. "I was thinking the same thing this morning. That dome begins to give a man the willies. How do the natives stand it? Or do they?"

Trimmer pulled out a cigar case. Murphy refused the offer.

"Local tobacco," said Trimmer. "Very good." He lit up thoughtfully. "Well, you might say that the Cirgameski are schizophrenic. They've got the docile Javanese blood, plus the Arabian élan. The Javanese part is on top, but every once in a while you see a flash of arrogance. . . . You never know. I've been out here nine years and I'm still a stranger." He puffed on his cigar, studied Murphy with his careful eyes. "You work for *Know Your Universe!*, I hear."

"Yeah. I'm one of the leg men."

"Must be a great job."

"A man sees a lot of the galaxy, and he runs into queer tales, like this sjambak stuff."

Trimmer nodded without surprise. "My advice to you, Murphy, is lay off the sjambaks. They're not healthy around here."

Murphy was startled by the bluntness. "What's the big mystery about these sjambaks?"

Trimmer looked around the room. "This place is bugged."

"I found two pick-ups and plugged 'em," said Murphy.

Trimmer laughed. "Those were just plants. They hide 'em where a man might just barely spot 'em. You can't catch the real ones. They're woven into the cloth—pressure-sensitive wires."

Murphy looked critically at the cloth walls.

"Don't let it worry you," said Trimmer. "They listen more out of habit than anything else. If you're fussy we'll go for a walk."

The road led past the palace into the country. Murphy and Trimmer sauntered along a placid river, overgrown with lily pads, swarming with large white ducks.

"This sjambak business," said Murphy. "Everybody talks around it. You can't pin anybody down."

"Including me," said Trimmer. "I'm more or less privileged around here. The Sultan finances his reclamation through the bank, on the basis of my reports. But there's more to Singhalût than the Sultan."

"Namely?"

Trimmer waved his cigar waggishly. "Now we're getting in where I don't like to talk. I'll give you a hint. Prince Ali thinks roofing-in more valleys is a waste of money, when there's Hadra and New Batavia and Sundaman so close."

"You mean—armed conquest?"

Trimmer laughed. "You said it, not me."

"They can't carry on much of a war—unless the soldiers commute by monorail."

"Maybe Prince Ali thinks he's got the answer."

"Sjambaks?"

"I didn't say it," said Trimmer blandly.

Murphy grinned. After a moment he said. "I picked up with a girl named Soek Panjoebang who plays the *gamelan*. I suppose she's working for either the Sultan or Prince Ali. Do you know which?"

Trimmer's eyes sparkled. He shook his head. "Might be either one. There's a way to find out."

"Yeah?"

"Get her off where you're sure there's no spy-cells. Tell her two things—one for Ali, the other for the Sultan. Whichever one reacts you know you've got her tagged."

"For instance?"

"Well, for instance she learns that you can rig up a hypnotic ray from a flashlight battery, a piece of bamboo, and a few lengths of wire. That'll get Ali in an awful sweat. He can't get weapons. None at all. And for the Sultan," Trimmer was warming up to his intrigue, chewing on his cigar with gusto, "tell her you're on to a catalyst that turns clay into aluminum and oxygen in the presence of sunlight. The Sultan would sell his right leg for something like that. He tries hard for Singhalût and Cirgamesç."

"And Ali?"

Trimmer hesitated. "I never said what I'm gonna say. Don't forget—I never said it."

"Okay, you never said it."

"Ever hear of a *jehad*?"

"Mohammedan holy wars."

"Believe it or not, Ali wants a *jehad*."

"Sounds kinda fantastic."

"Sure it's fantastic. Don't forget, I never said anything about it. But suppose someone—strictly unofficial, of course—let the idea percolate around the Peace Office back home."

"Ah," said Murphy. "That's why you came to see me."

TRIMMER TURNED a look of injured innocence. "Now, Murphy, you're a little unfair. I'm a friendly guy. Of course I don't like to see the bank lose what we've got tied up in the Sultan."

"Why don't you send in a report yourself?"

"I have! But when they hear the same thing from you, a *Know Your Universe!* man, they might make a move."

Murphy nodded.

"Well, we understand each other," said Trimmer heartily, "and everything's clear."

"Not entirely. How's Ali going to launch a *jehad* when he doesn't have any weapons, no warships, no supplies?"

"Now," said Trimmer, "we're getting into the realm of supposition." He paused, looked behind him. A farmer pushing a rotary tiller, bowed politely, trundled ahead. Behind was a young man in a black turban, gold earrings, a black and red vest, white pantaloons, black curl-toed slippers. He bowed, started past. Trimmer held up his hand. "Don't waste your time up there; we're going back in a few minutes."

"Thank you, Tuan."

"Who are you reporting to? The Sultan or Prince Ali?"

"The Tuan is sure to pierce the veil of my evasions. I shall not dissemble. I am the Sultan's man."

Trimmer nodded. "Now, if you'll kindly remove to about a hundred yards, where your whisper pick-up won't work."

"By your leave, I go." He retreated without haste.

"He's almost certainly working for Ali," said Trimmer.

"Not a very subtle lie."

"Oh, yes—third level. He figured I'd take it second level."

"How's that again?"

"Naturally I wouldn't believe him. He knew I knew that he knew it. So when he said 'Sultan', I'd think he wouldn't lie simply, but that he'd lie double—that he actually was working for the Sultan."

Murphy laughed. "Suppose he told you a fourth-level lie?"

"It starts to be a toss-up pretty soon," Trimmer admitted. "I don't think he gives me credit for that much subtlety. . . . What are you doing the rest of the day?"

"Taking footage. Do you know where I can find some picturesque rites? Mystical dances, human sacrifice? I've got to work up some glamor and exotic lore."

"There's this sjambak in the cage. That's about as close to the medieval as you'll find anywhere in Earth Commonwealth."

"Speaking of sjambaks . . ."

"No time," said Trimmer. "Got to get back. Drop in at my office—right down the square from the palace."

MURPHY RETURNED to his suite. The shadowy figure of his room servant said, "His Highness the Sultan desires the Tuan's attendance in the Cascade Garden."

"Thank you," said Murphy. "As soon as I load my camera."

The Cascade Room was an open patio in front of an artificial waterfall. The Sultan was pacing back and forth, wearing dusty khaki puttees, brown plastic boots, a yellow polo shirt. He carried a twig which he used as a riding crop, slapping his boots as he walked. He turned his head as Murphy appeared, pointed his twig at a wicker bench.

"I pray you sit down, Mr. Murphy." He paced once up and back. "How is your suite? You find it to your liking?"

"Very much so."

"Excellent," said the Sultan. "You do me honor with your presence."

Murphy waited patiently.

"I understand that you had a visitor this morning," said the Sultan.

"Yes. Mr. Trimmer."

"May I inquire the nature of the conversation?"

"It was of a personal nature," said Murphy, rather more shortly than he meant.

The Sultan nodded wistfully. "A Singhalûsi would have wasted an hour telling me half-truths—distorted enough to confuse, but not sufficiently inaccurate to anger me if I had a spy-cell on him all the time."

Murphy grinned. "A Singhalûsi has to live here the rest of his life."

A servant wheeled a frosted cabinet before them, placed goblets under two spigots, withdrew. The Sultan cleared his throat. "Trimmer is an excellent fellow, but unbelievably loquacious."

Murphy drew himself two inches of chilled rosy-pale liquor. The Sultan slapped his boots with the twig. "Undoubtedly he confided all my private business to you, or at least as much as I have allowed him to learn."

"Well—he spoke of your hope to increase the compass of Singhalût."

"That, my friend, is no hope; it's absolute necessity. Our population density is fifteen hundred to the square mile. We must expand or smother. There'll be too little food to eat, too little oxygen to breathe."

Murphy suddenly came to life. "I could make that idea the theme of my feature! Singhalût Dilemma: Expand or Perish!"

"No, that would be inadvisable, inapplicable."

Murphy was not convinced. "It sounds like a natural."

The Sultan smiled. "I'll impart an item of confidential information— although Trimmer no doubt has preceded me with it." He gave his boots an irritated whack. "To expand I need funds. Funds are best secured in an atmosphere of calm and confidence. The implication of emergency would be disastrous to my aims."

"Well," said Murphy, "I see your position."

The Sultan glanced at Murphy sidelong. "Anticipating your cooperation, my Minister of Propaganda has arranged an hour's program, stressing our progressive social attitude, our prosperity and financial prospects . . ."

"But, Sultan . . ."

"Well?"

"I can't allow your Minister of Propaganda to use me and *Know Your Universe!* as a kind of investment brochure."

The Sultan nodded wearily. "I expected you to take that attitude. . . . Well—what do you yourself have in mind?"

"I've been looking for something to tie to," said Murphy. "I think it's going to be the dramatic contrast between the ruined cities and the new domed valleys. How the Earth settlers succeeded where the ancient people failed to meet the challenge of the dissipating atmosphere."

"Well," the Sultan said grudgingly, "that's not too bad."

"Today I want to take some shots of the palace, the dome, the city, the paddies, groves, orchards, farms. Tomorrow I'm taking a trip out to one of the ruins."

"I see," said the Sultan. "Then you won't need my charts and statistics?"

"Well, Sultan, I could film the stuff your Propaganda Minister cooked up, and I could take it back to Earth. Howard Frayberg or Sam

Catlin would tear into it, rip it apart, lard in some head-hunting, a little cannibalism and temple prostitution, and you'd never know you were watching Singhalût. You'd scream with horror, and I'd be fired."

"In that case," said the Sultan, "I will leave you to the dictates of your conscience."

HOWARD FRAYBERG looked around the gray landscape of Riker's Planet, gazed out over the roaring black Mogador Ocean. "Sam, I think there's a story out there."

Sam Catlin shivered inside his electrically heated glass overcoat. "Out on that ocean? It's full of man-eating plesiosaurs—horrible things forty feet long."

"Suppose we worked something out on the line of Moby Dick? *The White Monster of the Mogador Ocean.* We'd set sail in a catamaran—"

"Us?"

"No," said Frayberg impatiently. "Of course not us. Two or three of the staff. They'd sail out there, look over these gray and red monsters, maybe fake a fight or two, but all the time they're after the legendary white one. How's it sound?"

"I don't think we pay our men enough money."

"Wilbur Murphy might do it. He's willing to look for a man riding a horse up to meet his space-ships."

"He might draw the line at a white plesiosaur riding up to meet his catamaran."

Frayberg turned away. "Somebody's got to have ideas around here. . . ."

"We'd better head back to the space-port," said Catlin. "We got two hours to make the Sirgamesk shuttle."

WILBUR MURPHY sat in the Barangipan, watching marionettes performing to xylophone, castanet, gong and *gamelan*. The drama had its roots in proto-historic Mohenjō-Darō. It had filtered down through ancient India, medieval Burma, Malaya, across the Straits of Malacca to Sumatra and Java; from modern Java across space to Cirgamesç, five thousand years of time, two hundred light-years of space. Somewhere along the route it had met and assimilated modern technology. Magnetic beams controlled arms, legs and bodies, guided the poses and posturings. The manipulator's face, by agency of clip, wire, radio control and minuscule selsyn, projected his scowl, smile, sneer or grimace to the peaked little face he controlled. The language was that of Old Java, which perhaps a third of the spectators understood. This portion did not include Murphy, and when the performance ended he was no wiser than at the start.

Soek Panjoebang slipped into the seat beside Murphy. She wore musician's garb: a sarong of brown, blue, and black *batik*, and a fantastic headdress of tiny silver bells. She greeted him with enthusiasm.

"Weelbrrr! I saw you watching. . . ."

"It was very interesting."

"Ah, yes." She sighed. "Weelbrrr, you take me with you back to Earth? You make me a great picturama star, please, Weelbrrr?"

"Well, I don't know about that."

"I behave very well, Weelbrrr." She nuzzled his shoulder, looked soulfully up with her shiny yellow-hazel eyes. Murphy nearly forgot the experiment he intended to perform.

"What did you do today, Weelbrrr? You look at all the pretty girls?"

"Nope. I ran footage. Got the palace, climbed the ridge up to the condensation vanes. I never knew there was so much water in the air till I saw the stream pouring off those vanes! And *hot*!"

"We have much sunlight; it makes the rice grow."

"The Sultan ought to put some of that excess light to work. There's a secret process. . . . Well, I'd better not say."

"Oh come, Weelbrrr! Tell me your secrets!"

"It's not much of a secret. Just a catalyst that separates clay into aluminum and oxygen when sunlight shines on it."

Soek's eyebrows rose, poised in place like a seagull riding the wind. "Weelbrrr! I did not know you for a man of learning!"

"Oh, you thought I was just a bum, eh? Good enough to make picturama stars out of *gamelan* players, but no special genius. . . ."

"No, no, Weelbrrr."

"I know lots of tricks. I can take a flashlight battery, a piece of copper foil, a few transistors and bamboo tube and turn out a paralyzer gun that'll stop a man cold in his tracks. And you know how much it costs?"

"No, Weelbrrr. How much?"

"Ten cents. It wears out after two or three months, but what's the difference? I make 'em as a hobby—turn out two or three an hour."

"Weelbrrr! You're a man of marvels! Hello! We will drink!"

And Murphy settled back in the wicker chair, sipping his rice beer.

* * * * *

"TODAY," said Murphy, "I get into a space-suit, and ride out to the ruins in the plain. Ghatamipol, I think they're called. Like to come?"

"No, Weelbrrr." Soek Panjoebang looked off into the garden, her hands busy tucking a flower into her hair. A few minutes later she said, "Why must you waste your time among the rocks? There are better things to do and see. And it might well be—dangerous." She murmured the last word off-handedly.

"Danger? From the sjambaks?"

"Yes, perhaps."

"The Sultan's giving me a guard. Twenty men with crossbows."

"The sjambaks carry shields."

"Why should they risk their lives attacking me?"

Soek Panjoebang shrugged. After a moment she rose to her feet. "Goodbye, Weelbrrr."

"Goodbye? Isn't this rather abrupt? Won't I see you tonight?"

"If so be Allah's will."

Murphy looked after the lithe swaying figure. She paused, plucked a yellow flower, looked over her shoulder. Her eyes, yellow as the flower, lucent as water-jewels, held his. Her face was utterly expressionless. She turned, tossed away the flower with a jaunty gesture, and continued, her shoulders swinging.

Murphy breathed deeply. She might have made picturama at that. . . .

One hour later he met his escort at the valley gate. They were dressed in space-suits for the plains, twenty men with sullen faces. The trip to Ghatamipol clearly was not to their liking. Murphy climbed into his own suit, checked the oxygen pressure gauge, the seal at his collar. "All ready, boys?"

No one spoke. The silence drew out. The gatekeeper, on hand to let the party out, snickered. "They're all ready, Tuan."

"Well," said Murphy, "let's go then."

Outside the gate Murphy made a second check of his equipment. No leaks in his suit. Inside pressure: 14.6. Outside pressure: zero. His twenty guards morosely inspected their crossbows and slim swords.

The white ruins of Ghatamipol lay five miles across Pharasang Plain. The horizon was clear, the sun was high, the sky was black.

Murphy's radio hummed. Someone said sharply, "Look! There it goes!" He wheeled around; his guards had halted, and were pointing. He saw a fleet something vanishing into the distance.

"Let's go," said Murphy. "There's nothing out there."

"Sjambak."

"Well, there's only one of them."

"Where one walks, others follow."

"That's why the twenty of you are here."

"It is madness! Challenging the sjambaks!"

"What is gained?" another argued.

"I'll be the judge of that," said Murphy, and set off along the plain. The warriors reluctantly followed, muttering to each other over their radio intercoms.

THE ERODED city walls rose above them, occupied more and more of the sky. The platoon leader said in an angry voice, "We have gone far enough."

"You're under my orders," said Murphy. "We're going through the gate." He punched the button on his camera and passed under the monstrous portal.

The city was frailer stuff than the wall, and had succumbed to the thin storms which had raged a million years after the passing of life. Murphy marvelled at the scope of the ruins. Virgin archaeological territory! No telling what a few weeks digging might turn up. Murphy considered his expense account. Shifkin was the obstacle.

There'd be tremendous prestige and publicity for *Know Your Universe!* if Murphy uncovered a tomb, a library, works of art. The Sultan would gladly provide diggers. They were a sturdy enough people; they could make quite a showing in a week, if they were able to put aside their superstitions, fears and dreads.

Murphy sized one of them up from the corner of his eye. He sat on a sunny slab of rock, and if he felt uneasy he concealed it quite successfully. In fact, thought Murphy, he appeared completely relaxed. Maybe the problem of securing diggers was a minor one after all. . . .

And here was an odd sidelight on the Singhalûsi character. Once clear of the valley the man openly wore his shirt, a fine loose garment of electric blue, in defiance of the Sultan's edict. Of course out here he might be cold. . . .

Murphy felt his own skin crawling. How could he be cold? How could he be alive? Where was his space-suit? He lounged on the rock, grinning sardonically at Murphy. He wore heavy sandals, a black turban, loose breeches, the blue shirt. Nothing more.

Where were the others?

Murphy turned a feverish glance over his shoulder. A good three miles distant, bounding and leaping toward Singhalût, were twenty desperate figures. They all wore space-suits. This man here . . . A sjambak? A wizard? A hallucination?

THE CREATURE rose to his feet, strode springily toward Murphy. He carried a crossbow and a sword, like those of Murphy's fleet-footed guards. But he wore no space-suit. Could there be breathable traces of an atmosphere? Murphy glanced at his gauge. Outside pressure: zero.

Two other men appeared, moving with long elastic steps. Their eyes were bright, their faces flushed. They came up to Murphy, took his arm. They were solid, corporeal. They had no invisible force fields around their heads.

Murphy jerked his arm free. "Let go of me, damn it!" But they certainly couldn't hear him through the vacuum.

He glanced over his shoulder. The first man held his naked blade a foot or two behind Murphy's bulging space-suit. Murphy made no further resistance. He punched the button on his camera to automatic. It would now run for several hours, recording one hundred pictures per second, a thousand to the inch.

The sjambaks led Murphy two hundred yards to a metal door. They opened it, pushed Murphy inside, banged it shut. Murphy felt the vibration through his shoes, heard a gradually waxing hum. His gauge showed an outside pressure of 5, 10, 12, 14, 14.5. An inner door opened. Hands pulled Murphy in, unclamped his dome.

"Just what's going on here?" demanded Murphy angrily.

Prince Ali-Tomás pointed to a table. Murphy saw a flashlight battery, aluminum foil, wire, a transistor kit, metal tubing, tools, a few other odds and ends.

"There it is," said Prince Ali-Tomás. "Get to work. Let's see one of these paralysis weapons you boast of."

"Just like that, eh?"

"Just like that."

"What do you want 'em for?"

"Does it matter?"

"I'd like to know." Murphy was conscious of his camera, recording sight, sound, odor.

"I lead an army," said Ali-Tomás, "but they march without weapons. Give me weapons! I will carry the word to Hadra, to New Batavia, to Sundaman, to Boeng-Bohôt!"

"How? Why?"

"It is enough that I will it. Again, I beg of you . . ." He indicated the table.

Murphy laughed. "I've got myself in a fine mess. Suppose I don't make this weapon for you?"

"You'll remain until you do, under increasingly difficult conditions."

"I'll be here a long time."

"If such is the case," said Ali-Tomás, "we must make our arrangements for your care on a long-term basis."

Ali made a gesture. Hands seized Murphy's shoulders. A respirator was held to his nostrils. He thought of his camera, and he could have laughed. Mystery! Excitement! Thrills! Dramatic sequence for *Know Your Universe!* Staff-man murdered by fanatics! The crime recorded on his own camera! See the blood, hear his death-rattle, smell the poison!

The vapor choked him. What a break! What a sequence!

"SIRGAMESK," said Howard Frayberg, "bigger and brighter every minute."

"It must've been just about in here," said Catlin, "that Wilbur's horseback rider appeared."

"That's right! Steward!"

"Yes, sir?"

"We're about twenty thousand miles out, aren't we?"

"About fifteen thousand, sir."

"Sidereal Cavalry! What an idea! I wonder how Wilbur's making out on his superstition angle?"

Sam Catlin, watching out the window, said in a tight voice, "Why not ask him yourself?"

"Eh?"

"Ask him for yourself! There he is—outside, riding some kind of critter. . . ."

"It's a ghost," whispered Frayberg. "A man without a space-suit. . . . There's no such thing!"

"He sees us. . . . Look. . . ."

Murphy was staring at them, and his surprise seemed equal to their own. He waved his hand. Catlin gingerly waved back.

Said Frayberg, "That's not a horse he's riding. It's a combination ram-jet and kiddie car with stirrups!"

"He's coming aboard the ship," said Catlin. "That's the entrance port down there. . . ."

* * * * *

WILBUR MURPHY sat in the captain's stateroom, taking careful breaths of air.

"How are you now?" asked Frayberg.

"Fine. A little sore in the lungs."

"I shouldn't wonder," the ship's doctor growled. "I never saw anything like it."

"How does it feel out there, Wilbur?" Catlin asked.

"It feels awful lonesome and empty. And the breath seeping up out of your lungs, never going in—that's a funny feeling. And you miss the air blowing on your skin. I never realized it before. Air feels like—like silk, like whipped cream—it's got texture. . . ."

"But aren't you cold? Space is supposed to be absolute zero!"

"Space is nothing. It's not hot and it's not cold. When you're in the sunlight you get warm. It's better in the shade. You don't lose any heat by air convection, but radiation and sweat evaporation keep you comfortably cool."

"I still can't understand it," said Frayberg. "This Prince Ali, he's a kind of a rebel, eh?"

"I don't blame him in a way. A normal man living under those domes has to let off steam somehow. Prince Ali decided to go out crusading. I think he would have made it too—at least on Cirgamesç."

"Certainly there are many more men inside the domes. . . ."

"When it comes to fighting," said Murphy, "a sjambak can lick twenty men in space-suits. A little nick doesn't hurt him, but a little nick bursts open a space-suit, and the man inside comes apart."

"Well," said the Captain. "I imagine the Peace Office will send out a team to put things in order now."

Catlin asked, "What happened when you woke up from the chloroform?"

"Well, nothing very much. I felt this attachment on my chest, but didn't think much about it. Still kinda woozy. I was halfway through decompression. They keep a man there eight hours, drop pressure on him two pounds an hour, nice and slow so he don't get the bends."

"Was this the same place they took you, when you met Ali?"

"Yeah, that was their decompression chamber. They had to make a sjambak out of me; there wasn't anywhere else they could keep me. Well, pretty soon my head cleared, and I saw this apparatus stuck to my chest." He poked at the mechanism on the table. "I saw the oxygen tank,

I saw the blood running through the plastic pipes—blue from me to that carburetor arrangement, red on the way back in—and I figured out the whole arrangement. Carbon dioxide still exhales up through your lungs, but the vein back to the left auricle is routed through the carburetor and supercharged with oxygen. A man doesn't need to breathe. The carburetor flushes his blood with oxygen, the decompression tank adjusts him to the lack of air-pressure. There's only one thing to look out for; that's not to touch anything with your naked flesh. If it's in the sunshine it's blazing hot; if it's in the shade it's cold enough to cut. Otherwise you're free as a bird."

"But—how did you get away?"

"I saw those little rocket-bikes, and began figuring. I couldn't go back to Singhalût; I'd be lynched on sight as a sjambak. I couldn't fly to another planet—the bikes don't carry enough fuel.

"I knew when the ship would be coming in, so I figured I'd fly up to meet it. I told the guard I was going outside a minute, and I got on one of the rocket-bikes. There was nothing much to it."

"Well," said Frayberg, "it's a great feature, Wilbur—a great film! Maybe we can stretch it into two hours."

"There's one thing bothering me," said Catlin. "Who did the steward see up here the first time?"

Murphy shrugged. "It might have been somebody up here skylarking. A little too much oxygen and you start cutting all kinds of capers. Or it might have been someone who decided he had enough crusading.

"There's a sjambak in a cage, right in the middle of Singhalût. Prince Ali walks past; they look at each other eye to eye. Ali smiles a little and walks on. Suppose this sjambak tried to escape to the ship. He's taken aboard, turned over to the Sultan and the Sultan makes an example of him. . . ."

"What'll the Sultan do to Ali?"

Murphy shook his head. "If I were Ali I'd disappear."

A loudspeaker turned on. "Attention all passengers. We have just passed through quarantine. Passengers may now disembark. Important: no weapons or explosives allowed on Singhalût!"

"This is where I came in," said Murphy.

THE END

ABOUT THE AUTHOR

John Holbrook Vance (born August 28, 1916 in San Francisco, California) is an American fantasy and science fiction author. Most of his work has been published under the name Jack Vance. He has also published 11 mysteries as John Holbrook Vance and 3 as Ellery Queen. Other pen names include Alan Wade, Peter Held, John van See, and Jay Kavanse.

Among his awards are: Hugo Awards, in 1963 for *The Dragon Masters* and in 1967 for *The Last Castle*; a Nebula Award in 1966, also for *The Last Castle*; the Jupiter Award in 1975; the World Fantasy Award in 1984 for life achievement and in 1990 for *Lyonesse: Madouc*; an Edgar (the mystery equivalent of the Nebula) for the best first mystery novel in 1961 for *The Man in the Cage*. In 1992, he was Guest of Honor at the WorldCon in Orlando, Florida; and in 1997 he was named a SFWA Grand Master. A 2009 profile in the *New York Times Magazine* described Vance as "one of American literature's most distinctive and undervalued voices."

Since his first published story ("The World-Thinker" in *Thrilling Wonder Stories*) in 1945, Vance has written over sixty books. Among his earliest published work is a set of fantasy stories written while he served in the merchant marine during World War II. They appeared in 1950, several years after Vance had started publishing science fiction in the pulp magazines, under the title *The Dying Earth*. (Vance's original title, used for the Vance Integral Edition, is *Mazirian the Magician*.)

Vance wrote many science fiction short stories in the late 1940s and through the 1950s for publication in magazines. Of his novels written during this period, a few were science fiction, but most were mysteries. Few were published at the time, but Vance continued to write mysteries into the early 1970s. In total, he wrote 15 novels outside of science fiction and fantasy, including the extended outline, *The Telephone Was Ringing in the Dark*, published only by the VIE, and three books published under the Ellery Queen pseudonym. Some of these are not mysteries—for example, *Bird Island*—and many fit uneasily in the category. These stories are set in and around his native San Francisco, except for one set in Italy and another in Africa. Two begin in San Francisco but take to the sea.

Many themes important to his more famous science fiction novels appeared first in the mysteries. The most obvious is the "book of dreams", which appears in *Bad Ronald* and *The View from Chickweed's*

Window, prior to being featured in *The Book of Dreams*. The revenge theme is also more prominent in certain mysteries than in the science fiction (*The View from Chickweed's Window* in particular). *Bad Ronald* was the only work by Vance ever to be made into film: a not particularly faithful TV movie aired on ABC in 1974, as well as a French production (*Méchant Garçon*) in 1992.

Certain of the science fiction stories are also mysteries. In addition to the comic *Magnus Ridolph* stories, two major stories feature the effectuator 'Miro Hetzel', a futuristic detective, and *Araminta Station* is largely concerned with solving various murders. Vance returned to the "Dying Earth" setting (a far distant future in which the sun is slowly going out, and magic and technology coexist) to write the picaresque adventures of the ne'er-do-well scoundrel Cugel the Clever, and those of the magician Rhialto the Marvellous. These books were written in 1963, 1978 and 1981. His other major fantasy work, *Lyonesse* (a trilogy including *Suldrun's Garden*, *The Green Pearl* and *Madouc*), was completed in 1989 and set on a mythological archipelago off the coast of France in the early Middle Ages.

The mystery and fantasy genres span his entire career.

Vance's stories written for pulps in the 1940s and 1950s cover many science fiction themes, with a tendency to emphasis on mysterious and biological themes (ESP, genetics, brain parasites, body switching, other dimensions, cultures) rather than technical ones. Robots, for example, are entirely absent. Many of the early stories are comic. By the 1960s, Vance had developed a futuristic setting which he came to call the "Gaean Reach". Thereafter, all his science fiction was, more or less explicitly, set therein. The Gaean Reach is loose and ever expanding. Each planet has its own history, state of development and culture. Within the Reach conditions tend to be peaceable and commerce tends to dominate. At the edges of the Reach, out in the lawless 'Beyond', conditions are sometimes, but not always, less secure.

SELECTED BIBLIOGRAPHY

Fantasy

The Dying Earth

The Dying Earth (author's preferred title *Mazirian the Magician*, collection of linked stories, 1950)

The Eyes of the Overworld (author's preferred title *Cugel the Clever*, novel 1966)

Cugel's Saga (author's preferred title *Cugel: The Skybreak Spatter-light*, novel, 1983)

Rhialto the Marvellous (collection of linked stories, 1984)

Lyonesse

Lyonesse: Suldrun's Garden (1983)

Lyonesse: The Green Pearl (1985) (vt *The Green Pearl*)

Lyonesse: Madouc (1989) (vt *Madouc*)

Science fiction

The Demon Princes Series

The Star King (1964)

The Killing Machine (1964)

The Palace of Love (1967)

The Face (1979)

The Book of Dreams (1981)

The Cadwal Chronicles

Araminta Station (1987)

Ecce and Old Earth (1991)

Throy (1992)

Alastor

Trullion: Alastor 2262 (1973)

Marune: Alastor 933 (1975)

Wyst: Alastor 1716 (1978)

Durdane

The Anome (alternate title: *The Faceless Man*, 1973)
The Brave Free Men (1973)
The Asutra (1974)

Tschai

City of the Chasch (author's preferred title: *The Chasch*. 1968)
Servants of the Wankh (reissue title: *The Wannek*, 1969)
The Dirdir (1969)
The Pnume (1970)

Non-series science fiction novels

The Five Gold Bands (alternate title: *The Space Pirate*, author's preferred title: *The Rapparee*) (1953)
Vandals of the Void (young adult novel) (1953)
To Live Forever (1956)
Big Planet (1957)
The Languages of Pao (1958)
Slaves of the Klau (original title: *Planet of the Damned*; alternate title: *Gold and Iron*) (1958)
Space Opera (1965)
The Blue World (1966)
Emphyrio (1969)
The Gray Prince (author's preferred title: *The Domains of Koryphon*) (1974)
Showboat World (author's preferred title: *The Magnificent Showboats of the Lower Vissel River, Lune XXIII, Big Planet*) (1975)
Maske: Thaery (1976)
Galactic Effectuator (this title is an editorial invention for the collected Miro Hetzel stories: "Freitzke's Turn" and "The Dogtown Tourist Agency") (1980)
Night Lamp (1996)
Ports of Call (1998)
Lurulu (2004; *Ports of Call* and *Lurulu* are parts 1 and 2 of the same novel)

Selected novellas

"Son of the Tree" (1951; re-issued as novel in 1964)
"Abercrombie Station" and "Cholwell's Chickens" (both 1952; two

linked novellas later issued as a novel, *Monsters in Orbit* (1965)

"Telek" (1952)

"The Houses of Iszm" (1954; re-issued as novel in 1964)

"The Moon Moth" (1961)

"Gateway to Strangeness" (1962) (vt Dust of Far Suns; Sail 25)

"The Dragon Masters" (1963 — Hugo Award Winner)

"The Brains of Earth" (author's preferred title: "Nopalgarth") (1966)

"The Last Castle" (1966, Nebula Award winner)

Mystery/Thrillers

Take My Face (1957, as by "Peter Held")

Isle of Peril (1957, as by "Alan Wade") (vt *Bird Isle*)

The Man In the Cage (1960)

The Four Johns (1964, as by "Ellery Queen"; vt *Four Men Called John* UK 1976)

A Room to Die In (1965, as by "Ellery Queen")

The Fox Valley Murders (1966)

The Madman Theory (1966, as by "Elrlery Queen")

The Pleasant Grove Murders (1967)

The Deadly Isles (1969)

Bad Ronald (1973)

The House on Lily Street: a Murder Mystery (1979)

Selected collections

Future Tense (1964)

The World Between and Other Stories (1965)

The Many Worlds of Magnus Ridolph (1966)

Eight Fantasms and Magics (1969)

Lost Moons (1982)

The Narrow Land (1982)

The Augmented Agent and Other Stories (1986)

The Dark Side of the Moon (1986)

Chateau D'If and Other Stories (1990)

When the Five Moons Rise (1992)

Tales of the Dying Earth (1999)

The Jack Vance Treasury (2006)

Autobiography

- *This Is Me, Jack Vance!* (Subterranean Press, 2009)

www.ingramcontent.com/pod-product-compliance
Lightning Source LLC
Chambersburg PA
CBHW050919120626
46552CB00004B/1653